Bridie Pruett

HOPE says

nope.

AuthorHouse™
1663 Liberty Drive
Bloomington, IN 47403
www.authorhouse.com
Phone: 1 (800) 839-8640

Published by AuthorHouse 10/31/2018

ISBN: 978-1-5462-6694-5 (sc)
ISBN: 978-1-5462-6693-8 (e)

Print information available on the last page.

This book is printed on acid-free paper.

authorHOUSE®

For Leyton and Parker.

You planted seeds of love in my heart that grew into an ivy of inspiration that I just couldn't contain any longer.

I bet you have a friend who is shy
like my friend Hope.

This is little Hope,
and her favorite
word is "Nope."

Hope said "nope" to everything she was too scared to do. Her friends tried to encourage her to try a few things new.

It's not that she was grouchy...

And it's not that she was mean...

But she wasn't happy either.

She was something in between.

They asked her to play ball, but the ball was moving fast.
She was afraid that she'd get hurt. That wouldn't be a blast.

They asked her to play trivia, but she did not like that game.
Hope thought she might get questions wrong and she would be ashamed.

Hope really did want to play, but she was just too shy.

Was she scared to be embarrassed?

Was that the reason why?

Her friends said,
"Hope, we love you! We do not think you're a dope!"
She tried to find some courage, but instead Hope just said,
"nope."

When she didn't feel like playing...

...she'd pet her dog Pup Pup. He was her tiny, yapper dog. He always cheered her up.

One day, she thought of all her friends
and how they all had fun.
She looked inside herself and thought of
all she had not done.

But then she watched
her Pup Pup, always
smiling without fail.

He never was unhappy,
and he always
wagged his tail.

Hope wished she could have fun
like him, she thought,
"What can I do?"
She knew he always yipped,
"Yup! Yup!"
So, she could say "Yup" too!

The next day when she saw
her friends and they asked her
to play,
She shouted out a great big
"Yup!"
and changed her life that day.

She grabbed a tiny pencil and she tapped it on her chin. "There's so much that I want to do, but where should I begin?"

Hope wrote down her hopes and dreams and put them in a list.
She pointed to the first one. "Why don't I just start with this?"

And just like that, adventure became Hope's new middle name.

Hope "Adventure" Robinson! She never was the same.

She climbed the highest cliffs with just her bare hands and a rope.

Her friends asked...

...and proudly Hope said,

nope!

She learned to try all kinds of foods.
Her favorite? Cantaloupe!

Her friends asked...

is
it
disgusting
?

...and proudly
Hope said,

nope!

broccoli

watermelon

cake

pretzel

pizza

eggplant

CANTALOUPE

She took a plane to Italy, and ate spaghetti with the Pope.

Her friends asked...

...and proudly Hope said,

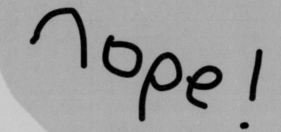

She traveled to the jungle
and she met an antelope!

Her friends asked...

...and proudly Hope said,

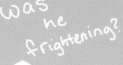

She made a circus friend who taught her how to walk tightrope.

Her friends asked...

...and proudly Hope said,

She drove up a mountain and went skiing down the slope.

They asked "Is there anymore you wanted to fulfill?"
Her head was stuffed with memories. Her face beamed with a thrill.

She tucked away her list of goals inside an envelope.
She looked down at her Pup Pup,
and proudly Hope said...

Bridie Pruett has a long career as an entrepreneur in the arts. However, her biggest achievement to date is getting both of her boys to sleep at the same time. Never shying away from a passion project, Bridie has always been a dreamer and a creator, and encourages young minds to create whenever and wherever they feel like creating and dreaming.

Printed in the United States
By Bookmasters